Crossing the New Bridge

EMILY ARNOLD McCULLY

G. P. PUTNAM'S SONS • NEW YORK

Copyright © 1994 by Emily Arnold McCully
All rights reserved. This book, or parts thereof,
may not be reproduced in any form without permission
in writing from the publisher.
G. P. Putnam's Sons, a division of The Putnam & Grosset Group,
200 Madison Avenue, New York, NY 10016.
G. P. Putnam's Sons, Reg. U.S. Pat. & Tm. Off.
Published simultaneously in Canada.
Printed in Hong Kong by South China Printing Co. (1988) Ltd.
Text set in Hadriano Light. Lettering by David Gatti
Library of Congress Cataloging-in-Publication Data
McCully, Emily Arnold. Crossing the new bridge /
by Emily Arnold McCully. p. cm.
Summary: When a new bridge is built over the river,
the happiest person in the town must be the first to cross it.
[1. Bridges—Fiction. 2. Happiness—Fiction.] I. Title.
PZ7.M478415Cr 1994 [E]—dc20 93-16047 CIP AC
ISBN 0-399-22618-4
10 9 8 7 6 5 4 3 2 1
First Impression

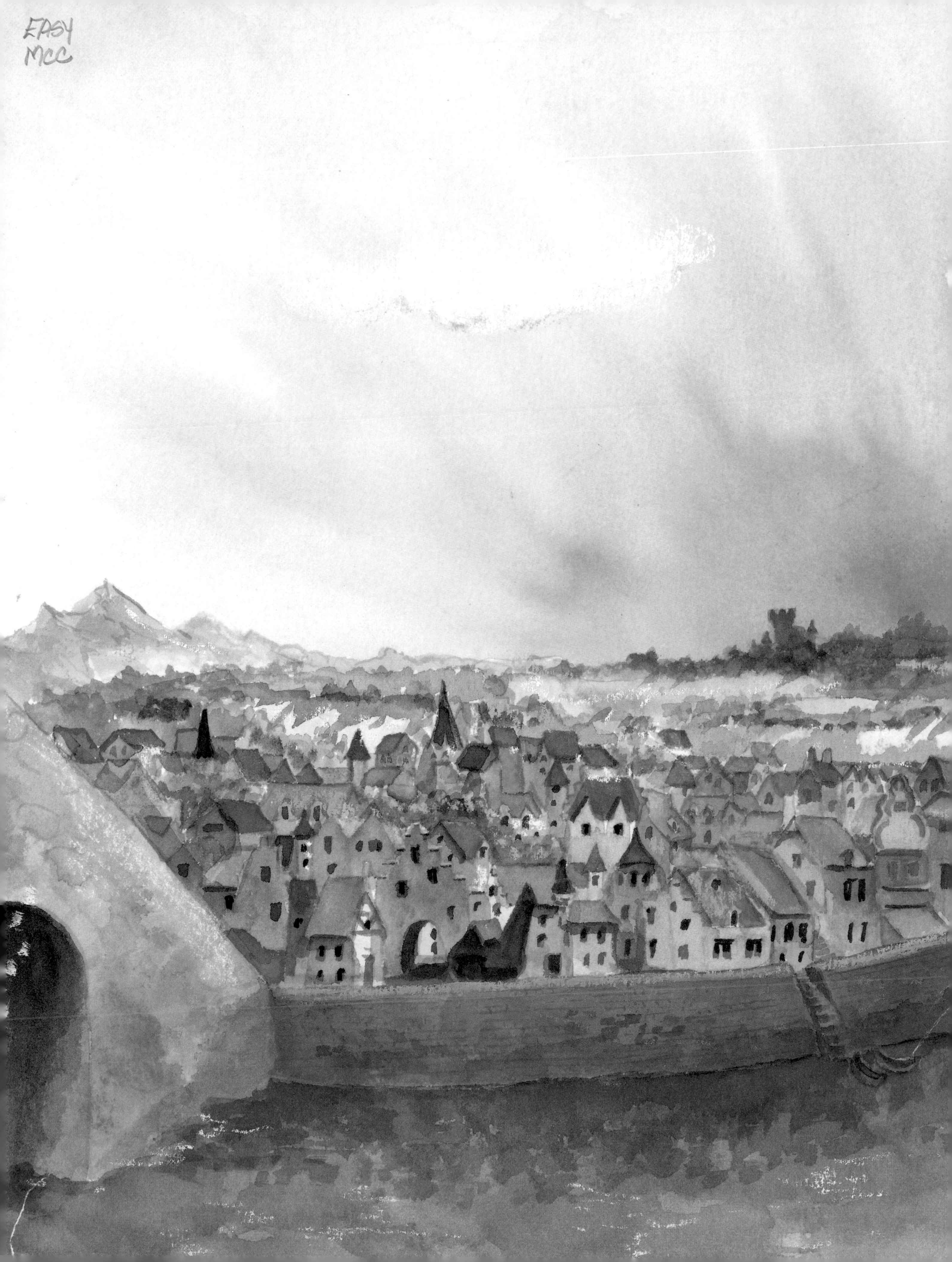

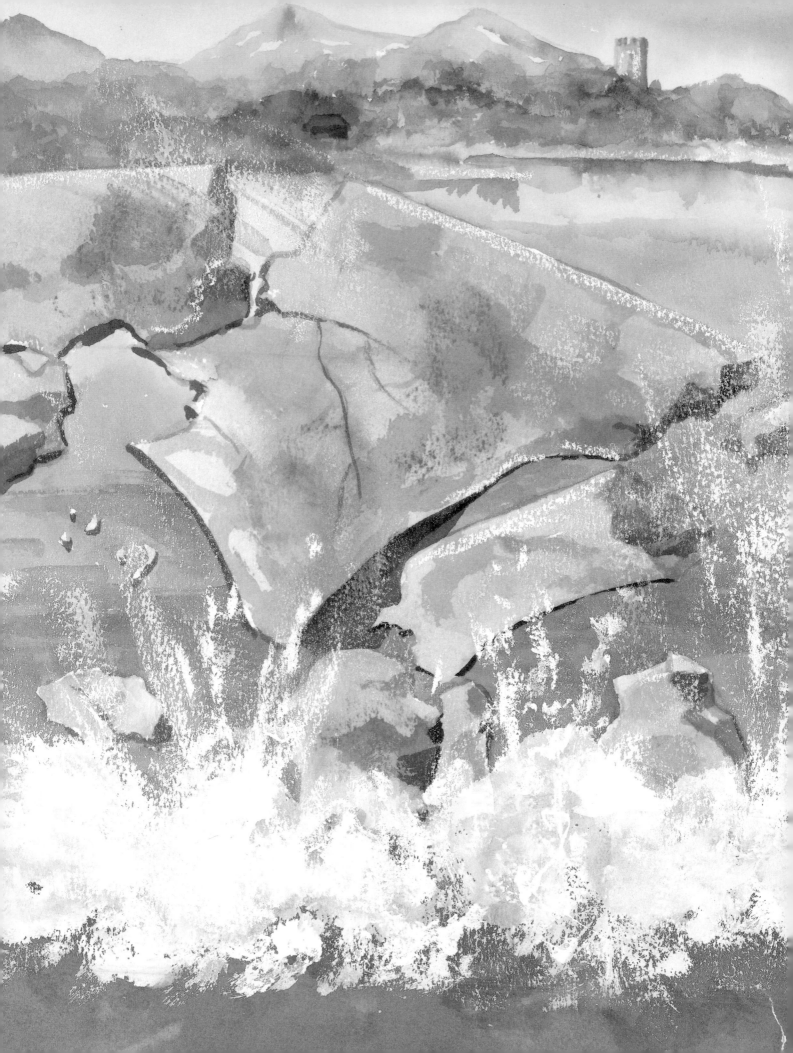

Long ago, in a town by the river, the Old Bridge suddenly creaked, cracked, and fell into the water.

The Mayor was among the first on the scene. "This is a calamity," he declared. "The town must have a bridge. We'll run out of food!"

"Someone will have to build a new one," said the Scribe.

"I was going to say that," said the Mayor. "Find a bridge builder."

"Ask the Jubilattis," said an old woman.

"*Ask the Jubilattis!*" thundered the Mayor. "Do I have to do all the thinking around here?"

In the midst of all the commotion, the Jubilattis arrived.
"Ah," said the Mayor. "Can you build us a new bridge?"
The Jubilattis laughed. "Of course we can!" said Mama Jubilatti.
"We can build anything," the family sang.

"Thank goodness!" said the Mayor. He began to plan his triumphal procession across the completed bridge.

But the old woman tugged at his sleeve. "What about our tradition?" she snapped. "The first person to cross a new bridge must be the happiest in town."

"The happiest person in town?" repeated the Mayor unhappily.

"That's right!" she cackled. "And furthermore, if anyone else crosses first, a CURSE WILL FALL ON ALL OF US!"

"*A curse!*" gasped the Mayor. "We can't have a curse while I am in office! How do we find this happiest person?"

Bang, bang came the sounds of the Jubilattis at work across the river.

"Well, we had better start looking, Your Honor," the Scribe said nervously.

The Mayor thought hard. "Let's try the Banker," he said. "He's richer than everyone else. He must be happier, too."

The Banker was in his vault, counting. "He seems happy," whispered the Scribe.

"Sir, we have chosen you to be the first—" the Mayor began.

"Not now, not now! One thousand twenty-six, one thousand twenty-seven..." muttered the Banker.

"Heave ho!" called one of the Jubilattis.

The Banker began to moan. "A sovereign is missing! Call the Sheriff!"

"Your Honor, this Banker is not really happy," whispered the Scribe.

"Let's try the Grocer," said the Mayor. "She is more beautiful than anyone else. Maybe she is happier, too."

The Grocer hummed as she arranged melons in her shop window.

"Tell us if you are happy, Madam," said the Mayor.

"What a question!" said the Grocer. "If you looked like me, wouldn't you be happy?" She smiled at her mirror.

Suddenly, she shrieked. "OH NO! OH HORRORS! There is a wrinkle on my forehead! And—ANOTHER! Don't look at me!"

"She isn't happy either," said the Mayor.

"Look at that bridge!" said the Scribe. "Those Jubilattis are *workers*!"

The Mayor groaned.

"LOOK!" he cried. "There is a poet. She must surely be happy."

"See here, are you happy?" he asked the Poet.

The Poet gazed at them. "Happy?" she mused. "Of course I am happy. The world is full of enchantment."

"Perfect!" crowed the Mayor. "We've found her!"

Then he noticed that a tear was rolling down the Poet's cheek, followed by another. "But what's the matter?" he asked.

"I am only a poet," said the Poet. "I can never write verse as perfect as this rosebud."

The Mayor wiped his forehead. "We must press on," he said.

"Your Honor," said the Scribe. "There is a mother with twelve healthy children living right up this street. She must be happy!"

"Lead me to her!" said the Mayor.

Over the rooftops, the bridge marched steadily across the river. The Jubilattis never slowed their work.

The Mayor knocked and knocked and finally a child opened the door.

"Where is your mother?" asked the Mayor.

"She's fishing for my shoes. Aggie threw them down the well," said the child.

"Fetch her, please. Tell her the Mayor is here."

"Madam," he said, when she had come, "are you happy?"

"WHAT'S THAT?" asked the Mother. "SPEAK UP!"

"WE ARE LOOKING FOR THE HAPPIEST PERSON IN TOWN!" shouted the Mayor.

"Well, any other day that could be me," said the Mother. "But today

one of my boys chased another up that tree and he fell down the chimney and while I was borrowing a ladder so I could go after him, the soup boiled over. The baby ran out and opened the gate and the cow ran away. This one couldn't run after it because her sister threw her shoes down the well before she broke the bed, jumping on it."

"Thank you," said the Mayor. "We are sorry to have interrupted you."

To the Scribe he said, "*Somebody* in this town must be happier than the rest of us!"

As they walked up the street, they could clearly hear Mama Jubilatti say, "Son, give me a hand with this plank."

"They are past the middle of the river!" said the Scribe. "What a beauty that bridge will be!"

"We can't waste our time admiring the bridge," grumbled the Mayor. "Get a good night's sleep."

In the days that followed, as the bridge came nearer and nearer their shore, the Mayor and the Scribe continued to search high and low. But no one seemed happier than anyone else.

The Pie Seller had blisters on her feet; the Apothecary had mixed up

the hiccup potion with the dropsy potion; the Barber had nicked the Miller's chin; the Ragpicker missed her mother, who lived across the river; and so on.

"Oh dear, oh dear," said the Mayor. "*I* used to be happy myself."

That afternoon, a great cheer rose from the riverbank. "WE DID IT!" shouted the Jubilattis.

"It was hard work," said Papa.

"But well worth it," said Mama.

"I think it's our best bridge," said the son.

"It is an excellent bridge," said the Mayor miserably.

The Jubilattis beamed.

"But we can't use it," said the Mayor.

"*Can't use it?*" cried the Jubilattis.

"Tradition says the happiest person in town must cross it first."

"Very good," said Mama.

"But we couldn't *find* the happiest person," said the Scribe.

"A moment ago, WE were the happiest people in town," said Papa.

"You were?" asked the Mayor.

"Of course! We built the best bridge of our lives!"

"Then why aren't you happy now?"

"Because you can't use it," said Mama.

"But, Mama," said the daughter, "we have already crossed the bridge!"
Everyone looked at everyone else.
"YOU'RE RIGHT!" cried the Mayor. "You're right, you're right, you're right, you're right!"

A cheer rose again and then everyone in the town scampered onto the bridge, where they danced back and forth from shore to shore.

The Mayor even danced with the old woman. He was so happy that he forgave her for bringing up the ancient tradition in the first place.

The Jubilattis, of course, had been happy all along.